Weekly Reader Books Presents

The Bear Next Door

by Ida Luttrell
pictures by Sarah Stapler

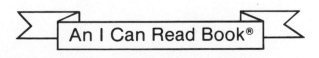

An I Can Read Book®

HarperCollins*Publishers*

This book is a presentation of Weekly Reader Books. Weekly Reader Books offers book clubs for children from preschool through high school. For further information write to: **Weekly Reader Books,** 4343 Equity Drive, Columbus, Ohio 43228.

Published by arrangement with HarperCollins Publishers. Weekly Reader is a federally registered trademark of Field Publications.

I Can Read Book is a registered trademark of HarperCollins Publishers.
The Bear Next Door
Text copyright © 1991 by Ida Luttrell
Illustrations copyright © 1991 by Sarah A. Stapler
Printed in the U.S.A. All rights reserved.
1   2   3   4   5   6   7   8   9   10
First Edition

Library of Congress Cataloging-in-Publication Data
Luttrell, Ida.
   The Bear next door / by Ida Luttrell ; pictures by Sarah Stapler.
       p.   cm. — (An I can read book)
   Summary: Three episodes in the developing friendship of Vic Bear and
Arlo Gopher demonstrate how they are good neighbors.
ISBN 0-06-024023-7. — ISBN 0-06-024024-5 (lib. bdg.)
   [1. Neighborliness—Fiction.   2. Friendship—Fiction.   3. Bears—
Fiction.   4. Gophers—Fiction.]   I. Stapler, Sarah, ill.
II. Title.   III. Series.
PZ7.L97953Bg   1991   90-4153
[E]—dc20   CIP
                                                                 AC

The illustrations in this book are rendered in watercolor and pen and ink.

·CONTENTS·

Moving Day · 6

Once Upon a Time · 24

Blueberry Frost · 44

Moving Day

One hot summer day
Arlo Gopher went outside
to turn on his sprinkler.
Someone was moving in next door.

"Great," Arlo said.

"I will be a good neighbor

and say hello."

7

But no one came to the door

when Arlo knocked,

so Arlo went home.

He turned on his sprinkler

and went inside.

Soon he heard the doorbell ring.

Arlo opened the door.

"Hello," Arlo said.

"My name is Arlo.

Are you my new neighbor?"

"Yes, I am Vic Bear," said the bear.

"Would you move your sprinkler,

my furniture is getting wet."

"I am so sorry," said Arlo.

"I will take care of it."

"Thanks," Vic said, and left.

Arlo moved the sprinkler.

"What a way to meet a new neighbor!"
he said to himself.

Vic huffed by.

He had a box in his hands

and a dark look on his face.

Arlo tried to cheer him up.

"They say, 'Good fences

make good neighbors,'" he said.

Just then

the bottom fell out of Vic's box.

Cans and jars rolled into the mud.

Vic kicked the box across the yard.

"I have had it!" he roared.

"I am so sorry," Arlo cried.

"I will help you."

Arlo picked up the cans and jars.

He helped Vic move furniture

and unpack boxes.

They were hot and tired

when they finished.

"Thanks for helping," Vic said.

"Now for a nice bath."

"I know something better," said Arlo.

"Come with me."

Vic followed Arlo

to Arlo's backyard.

Arlo flopped down on the grass
under the sprinkler.
Vic flopped down on the grass too.

The fresh cool water

sprayed over them.

"Aaah," Vic said. "I must admit

good sprinklers make good neighbors!"

23

Once Upon a Time

One snowy night

Arlo went outside to get firewood.

The wind blew his door shut.

Arlo was locked out.

He went to Vic's house.

"I locked myself out," Arlo said.

"Would you help me open a window?"

"It is too cold and dark," said Vic.

"Why don't you spend the night here?"

"Thanks," said Arlo. "I will."

They sat by the fire.

"What do you like to do when

it is dark and snowy?" asked Arlo.

"Eat," said Vic.

"I like to read," said Arlo.

"Here is an old magazine,"

said Vic.

Arlo turned the pages.

"Here's a story called

'Little Pig on Roller Skates.'"

"Read it out loud," said Vic.

Vic began to toast marshmallows.

Arlo began to read.

"Once upon a time

Little Pig went to Big Pig's house

at the top of a hill.

They put on their roller skates

and skated in front of the house.

"Little Pig saw a path
that curved down the hill.
'Where does that path go?'
asked Little Pig.

" 'Don't go there!' Big Pig cried.

But it was too late.

Little Pig's skates took her

down the path and around the curve.

"She flew faster and faster;

she could not stop.

'Help!' she cried."

Arlo quickly turned the page.

"Oh, no!" he cried.

"The rest of the story is missing."

"I must have used it

to start the fire," said Vic.

"Now we will never know

what happened to Little Pig,"

Arlo said.

"Who cares?" said Vic.

"Have a marshmallow."

"How can you eat

at a time like this?" Arlo cried.

"Easy," said Vic.

"Let's play cards.

One for you. One for me."

"Look, Vic!" said Arlo.

"There are pigs on these cards.

I can't forget Little Pig!"

Vic threw down his cards.

"I am going to bed," he cried.

"You can go to bed

or stay up and worry.

Suit yourself!"

Vic stomped off to bed.

He climbed into the top bunk

and went to sleep.

Arlo crawled into the bottom bunk.

He turned over and over.

The bed creaked and woke Vic.

"What are you doing?" Vic yelled.

"I can't sleep

because of Little Pig," said Arlo.

"It is just a story," said Vic.

"Make up an ending for it."

"You do it," said Arlo.

Vic began.

"Little Pig cried, 'HELP!'

But Big Pig could not save her,

and she went over the cliff."

"Was she killed?" Arlo cried.

Vic grinned and said,

"She landed in a bin of marshmallows

next to the marshmallow factory,

and they let her eat all

the marshmallows that she squashed."

Arlo laughed.

"I like that ending, Vic."

He snuggled deep under the covers.

"Hey, Vic," he said,

"good storytellers

make good neighbors."

Blueberry Frost

One day in late spring

Vic hurried to Arlo's back door.

"My freezer won't freeze," he said.

"Will you keep this ice cream for me?"

"Sure," said Arlo.

"It is blueberry frost," Vic said.

"Guard it with your life!"

"It will be safe with me," Arlo said.

"I wonder if blueberry frost

is as good as my

crunchy nut marble fudge ice cream.

Mmm! This is good!"

One taste led to another.

When the moon came out that night,

the carton was empty

and Arlo's belly was full.

The next morning

Arlo ran to Herb's market.

He opened the ice cream chest.

He found almond ice cream

and peach ice cream.

He dug out vanilla and chocolate.

"There's no blueberry frost!"

he cried.

"Is that right?" said Herb.

"Do you have any blueberries?"

Arlo asked.

"Nope," said Herb.

"Oh, brother!" Arlo said.

He bought a box of raisins

and a carton of vanilla ice cream.

Arlo went home and mixed
the raisins and ice cream.

He stuffed it all

in the blueberry frost carton.

"Vic will hate me

when he finds out," Arlo said.

He put the ice cream away

just in time.

Vic was at the door.

"Get the bowls out, Arlo.

You are in for a treat,"

Vic said.

Vic started toward the freezer.

"Wait, Vic!" cried Arlo.

But Vic took out the ice cream

and filled the bowls.

"This looks funny," said Vic.

He took a bite.

"It *tastes* strange.

You taste it, Arlo."

Arlo took a small taste.

He could not look at Vic.

"Maybe the blueberries went bad

in my freezer," he said.

"Maybe so," said Vic.

"They taste like raisins."

Arlo could not stand it anymore.

"It's because they *are* raisins!"

he shouted. "I ate all

your blueberry frost ice cream!"

"You did what?" Vic roared.

"Do you hate me?" Arlo asked.

Vic looked hard at Arlo and sighed.

"No," he said.

"Will you ever trust me again?"
Arlo asked.

"Not with blueberry frost ice cream!"
Vic said, and he got up to go.

"Wait, Vic," Arlo said,

and he ran to his freezer.

"Here is some

crunchy nut marble fudge ice cream

that I made."